AF441787

DEDICATION

To April

Your continuous support and encouragement
mean so very much to me.
Thank you, my friend.

Much Love,
CK Marie

FINDING ME
a Take My Control Novella

*Must read Take My Control before reading Finding Me.

*Trigger Warning - This book contains content of abuse, drug use, strong sexual content (M/F, F/F) and adult language.
ALL sexual contents IS consensual.

EPILOGUE

TORI-16 YEARS OLD

Two weeks, I scream inside my head. Two weeks and I'll be out of this hellhole.

The only good thing my piece of shit father has done for me is allowing me to get my license… but it's not for my benefit. No, it's purely for him.

Most times he's to strung out to drive and even though I've been driving him around since I was thirteen, my father listened to me when I told him we shouldn't chance getting caught now that I'm sixteen.

Today is my test, and what luck, my father is coherent enough to take me.

Two more weeks, I whisper to myself.

I passed my test with flying colors. I knew I would. I had to, there's too much at stake if I failed.

I walk into the house and turn towards the hallway that leads to my bedroom.

"Where the fuck do you think you're going?"

My father's hand grips my arm tight, and he pulls me towards him before shoving my face into the wall. "That little piece of plastic doesn't mean you're free to do as you please. I have people coming over tonight. Get this fucking house cleaned up," he spins me around and moves his hand to my face. My jaw tight in his grip. "And you better be on your best behavior and do as you are told tonight," his upper lip curls up. "If you know what's good for you."

He pushes my face away, hard, sending me flying back into the wall once more.

I hold back my tears.

Two more weeks, I cry out in my head.

I glance at the clock on the stove. Seven o'clock. That gives me about an hour. No one ever shows until after eight.

My father is passed out on the couch. An empty beer bottle lays across his chest, a half-smoked joint sits in the ashtray.

How easy it would be to take that bottle and crack open his head.

I smile at the thought.

No, I can't do that. As much as I'd love to end him, I can't. They'd know it was me. I have to stick with my plan.

Quietly, I walk past the couch and go to my room. I lay down on the bed. I'm so tired.

Just a few minutes, I tell myself and close my eyes.

"Mommy!" I scream and grab onto her legs. She pushes me away, making me fall. Her hands reach down, but not for me. Instead, she picks up her suitcases. One in each hand.

I crawl to her and latch onto her ankle.

"Mommy, please don't leave me."

I lookup with my tear-filled eyes. She looks angry.

"Please Mommy, take me with you."

She kicks her leg out; I lose my grip, and the force of her kick knocks me back.

Setting her suitcases down, she kneels in front of me.

"I never wanted children," she says. "I never wanted this life. I. Never. Wanted. You."

She stands and picks up her suitcases again. I make one last attempt to hold on to her leg.

"Mommy."

The fist that hits my face is hard and has little white dots floating in front of my eyes.

"I'm not your Mommy," are the last words I hear before the door slams shut.

I jolt up out of bed. My body is trembling and I can feel the tears running down my cheeks.

It's been years since I've had that nightmare. When my Mom left, I was only eight years old. That nightmare invaded my sleep every night for months.

I hate her for what she did. She should have just killed me, but she knew that would've been mercy. So, instead, she left me… in HELL.

CHAPTER ONE

TORI
16 YEARS OLD – ONE WEEK TO GO

It's Friday night, I've cleaned the house as I do every Friday before everyone gets here.

My father just got into the shower. He never takes long, so I need to hurry.

I tip-toe down the hallway, stopping when I reach his room. Quietly, I open his bedroom door. As always, the bottles sit on the nightstand next to the bed.

There's only one I need. Carefully, I press down on the child-resistant tab and remove the cap. Tilting the bottle, I let one pill fall into my hand.

Ambien, I've been collecting them for two months now. One a week from him and if I'm lucky, his trashy friends leave one lying around after a night of partying.

This will be the last time I must sneak into his room and steal from him. I put the bottle back in its place and hurry back to my room.

Opening my closet door, I reach down and move the shoebox away from the corner. My fingers pull on the carpet that's tucked under the trim, it easily gives way and I fold it back revealing my little hideaway spot.

I pull out the small zipper bag and toss the pill in with the rest before covering back up my spot.

"Tori!"

My father's scream vibrates through my door.

The list of things he gave me to do runs through my head. I didn't forget. I did everything.

I rush to the door and out of my room, not giving him a chance to come and find me.

He's in the kitchen, standing in front of the bottles of liquor I had set out on the counter.

"What the fuck is this doing out here?"

Shit!

He grabs the bottle of Grey Goose.

"Do you think my asshole friends are worthy of this bottle?" It's not a question, and his voice is full of rage.

"I'm sorry."

The blow to my cheek feels like a wrecking ball.

"You're a worthless cunt like your mother."

I cringe at his words. I'm nothing like her. I would never leave my child with a monster.

I stand in the corner of the living room. The lights are dim, just bright enough to see my surroundings. I don't dare move unless I'm called upon.

Thankfully, everyone is focused on the lines of blow my father has stretched out across the table.

I close my eyes, not wanting to watch them.
One more week, I say to myself.
"Hey, girl."
Someone yells through the noise. I try to block out the surrounding sounds, taking my thoughts to where my life will be heading.
"Hey, Girl!"
The voice booms through the room, and a sharp pain hits my chest. I jump and my eyes fly open just in time to see the ashtray bounce off me and hit the floor.

My father stands and moves towards me, getting up in my face.
"What did I tell you about behaving tonight?" he scolds.

I don't respond; I know from experience that will only piss him off even more.
"Carter."
One woman on the couch calls my father's name.

She's been here several times. I don't remember her name, but I remember she'll do anything with any of the men… my father included, to get the drugs she wants.

I watch as she gets up and makes her way over to me.

I don't like the way she looks at me. A feeling of unease weighs down on me.

"Come with me, darling."

She takes my arm and pulls me away from my father.

I'm squeezed between this woman and a guy named Sonny, he's a regular here every weekend.

Soft fingers run across my cheek. This woman turns my head towards her.

"You're beautiful," she tells me. "I don't think your Dad realizes if he wants you to act like an adult, you need to be treated as one."

Bile rises in my throat and I swallow it down.

I know what she's thinking. I can see it in her eyes.

"Margo!" my father screams. "Get your fucking hands off of her!"

"Oh, Carter, I was just going to have some fun."

His rage heats the room. He grabs Margo by the hair.

"I will fucking rip your cunt to shreds and I won't be using my cock to do it!" he growls then turns to me.

My head is pulled back, he fists my hair in his hand.

"Get your fucking ass in your room. NOW!"

He drags me over the back of the couch and throws me towards the hallway.

I should be thankful he doesn't allow any of them to touch me sexually, but I know it's not out of love for me. No, it's because he is afraid one of his piece of shit, dumbass friends would talk.

One more week, I think to myself as I walk into my room.

Laying in my bed I let my hand travel, it's one way I know how to take away the pain that aches my body every day.

I'm no prude and definitely not a virgin, but I've only ever been with boys from school. They have become one of my escapes from this reality I call Hell.

The first time happened about six months ago… on a Monday, to be exact.

That weekend was the usual house full of drunks, druggies, and… sex. I had watched the men and women make out, even two women doing the same. There was always touching and grabbing, but that weekend had changed.

I don't know what that piece of shit Sonny brought, but the women were all over the men.

Usually, I'd look away when they would start making out, but what happened that weekend had me feeling things like never before.

The abuse I take from my father is physical and verbal. He never leaves a mark I can't hide… especially during the school year. And surprisingly he has never broken a bone in my body.

His threats of what he would do to me if I told anyone were ones that kept me silent.

There are nights I go to bed barely able to move.

One night I had taken a punch to the stomach that knocked the air right out of my lungs. The pain was so bad I couldn't breathe.

That was also the night I forgot about the pain. That was the night I first pleasured myself.

But it was that weekend when Sonny brought something different to the party… that weekend changed everything.

None of the assholes ever had sex outside of the bedrooms, but that weekend, whatever those women took had them spreading their legs right there in the living room.

I watched from my corner as the men did things to them that shocked and terrified me.

At first, I thought they were hurting the women, but I was so very wrong.

The look on every women's face and the sounds that escaped their mouths was not one of pain.

They were enjoying it, enjoying each other.

That was the weekend that changed everything for me.

When I arrived at school on Monday, I sought the one boy I knew would give me what I wanted… what I needed.

I lost my virginity that day after school to a stoner named Mitch in the back of-the-art supply room.

That day I found that adding pleasure to my pain made me forget… everything.

CHAPTER TWO

TORI
16 YEARS OLD – TWO DAYS LEFT

Today is Wednesday, July 1st. My father has a big party planned for the weekend. Not that there isn't a party every weekend, but this is the Fourth of July and the shit neighborhood we live in has one big street party or drug-fest as I like to call it.

I have a list of things to pick up at the grocery store, but most importantly I'm meeting Mitch beforehand to pick up an order… one that will change my future.

One good thing about my neighborhood is you can get practically anything you need… if it's in the form of drugs, weapons, or what I ordered… a fake ID. Another good thing is that no one asks questions, as long as you have the cash… and in my case, Ambien.

Mitch's brother is the master of fake ID's which is why I have no problem paying him two hundred dollars and a bag of pills.

Getting the money was tricky. The only times my father gives me money is when I'm grocery shopping or if I need something for school, and that includes clothing.

My father doesn't want attention brought our way, so make sure I have decent clothes and shoes to wear to school, lunch money so I can eat, and always pay school fees.

So I've been stealing money from him and his friends. Little by little every weekend and I now have enough to put my plan in action.

"You got my money and pills?" Donny asks me as he waves the ID in front of my face.

Reaching into the front pocket of my jeans, I pull out the two hundred bucks and the little bag of pills. He snatches it out of my hand and tosses the piece of plastic on the table.

It looks exactly like my driver's license, except with this one I'm twenty-one… not sixteen.

I slip my future into my pocket.

"Thank you, Donny."

"Yep," is all he says without looking up from the pile of cash he's sorting out.

"Aren't you forgetting something?" Mitch says as he steps up behind me. "You and I have a little business to finish," his hand traces down my spine stopping at my ass. "I hooked you up with my brother, now it's time to collect my fee." His hand grips my ass cheek.

"I have little time," I tell him. "I need to get back before my dad gets suspicious."

"Don't worry baby, it won't take long with your fine ass," his grip tightens, and he pushes me forward towards his room.

I took way too long. I pull in my driveway, throwing the car in park and rushing out and around to the trunk to grab the bags of groceries.

My father is sitting on the couch when I walk in the front door.

"Where the fuck have you been?" his voice full of anger and he points to the clock.

"The store was busy, everyone is shopping for the fourth," no lie about that. "And they didn't have the hot dogs you like, so I went to the store on the other side of town," again no lie.

I drop the bags on the kitchen table, then slip my purse strap off my shoulder. Grabbing out the two receipts and his change, I walk into the living room.

"Here," I hand it all to him.

He unfolds each receipt. I watch his eyes scan each one, then look at the clock again.

I can't lie to him. He always checks the time printed on the receipt.

I learned that lesson the hard way. That's why I went to go see Mitch and Donny first.

He tosses them and his change on the table and goes back to the show he's watching without saying another word.

My cue to put groceries away and make dinner.

After cleaning the kitchen, I take a shower to wash away the remnants of Mitch.

Feeling fresh, the scent of lavender coating my skin, I wrap my hair in a towel and head to my room.

My feet come to a halt when I step through the door.

Margo is sitting on my bed.

"What are you doing in here?" my words are shaky as the feeling of unease returns.

"Just want to talk," she smiles. "Your dad is passed out, you don't have to worry," she adds as if she's reading my mind.

"I'm tired and there's nothing you and I need to talk about."

She stands and walks over to me; her arm stretches out, shutting the door.

"Oh, but we do," her lips close to my ear and I panic. "I was driving down Collette Street earlier today."

I feel the sweat bubbling to the surface of my skin. *This can't be happening.*

"At first I thought it was Carter, but then I saw you and guess what else I saw?"

"I… I stopped t… to say hi to a fr… friend," my words stutter.

"Oh, honey, I know what type of friend the Gunder brothers are," Margo says and my body stiffens when I feel her tongue lick below my ear.

"Wh… what do you want?"

"Nothing tonight, sweetheart. But don't worry, I'll let you know and you will give me what I ask for," she presses her mouth to my ear. "Soon." She says, then turns and leaves my room.

Fuck!

This can't be happening. If she says anything to my father, my plan is shot.

CHAPTER THREE

TORI
16 YEARS OLD – THE DAY

I did not sleep after Margo left my room Wednesday night. Yesterday I felt like I was coming undone. Every time I heard a car, I panicked thinking it was her.

I was on pins and needles all day. Restless and terrified when people started showing up last night at the house. Margo never showed, but that didn't give me any peace and I had another sleepless night.

I'm exhausted today, but I need to focus. I only need to make it through the day, and I pray that today isn't the day Margo takes what she wants from me.

Our street is packed. Lawn chairs are scattered in everyone's yards. Tables set up with food and alcohol. It will be a weekend of hard-partying.

People passed out or puking on the lawns, having sex on the lawn… hell, I've seen it all happen on the sidewalks and in the streets.

There will be fights… lots of fights. The cops never come to our neighborhood. Unless someone is dead, they stay clear.

I just need to make it through another few hours. I have two duffle bags packed. Clothes, shoes, a few personal items, and cash. Eight hundred dollars, to be exact. Between what I took from my father and his friends when they were all passed out, either to drugged up or drunk to notice and add in all I saved during the school year by skipping lunch. I collected a thousand bucks, two of it going towards my new ID… *money well spent.*

I'm sitting on our rundown porch watching people go from house to house. A beer can or a plastic cup full of God knows what in one hand, a cigarette or joint in the other.

A high pitch scream pierces through the light breeze. I look a few houses down. A topless girl is being sprayed with a water hose. The men standing near are all whooping and hollering as she jumps up and down, her tits bouncing freely.

"Hey, baby doll."

A voice startles me.

"Jesus, Mitch! Don't sneak up on me like that."

"I wasn't sneaking, I walked right up the steps," he sits in the chair next to me. "You still needing a ride tonight?"

"Shh… keep your voice down," I look through the screen door, my father isn't in sight. "Yes, I do, please. Do you remember where I told you to park?"

"Yep. So, what's going on? You haven't told me anything except what you need me to do."

"I just need to take care of some things."

"At midnight?" he questions me, suspicion in his voice.

"Mitch I can't get into this right now. Just trust me, please."

"Fine, for now."

I hate not telling him. Mitch is a nice guy and the only true friend I have. But I can't chance a slip-up, especially now that I'm so close.

"Thank you," I tell him and reach for his hand. "I owe you."

"What the fuck is this?"

My father swings the screen door open. I pull my hand away from Mitch.

"We're just talking dad."

"Shut the fuck up!"

The backhand across my face stings. I see Mitch clench his fists.

"You boy, better keep away from my daughter and that goes for your fucking brother too!"

Mitch knows how my father is and makes the smart decision to back away. Once he's off the porch, my father turns back to me.

"Little slut," he grabs my arm pulling me out of the chair then shoves me into the house. "Spreading your legs for the Gunder brother?"

I keep my mouth shut. Anything I say will only add fuel to the fire. I let him bitch and I stay silent.

ELEVEN-THIRTY PM…

I avoided my father the entire evening, but stayed in sight so he could see me doing… nothing. The only people I talked to were a few girls from the neighborhood.

Everyone is fucked up. I knew they would be, that's why I wanted to wait to make my move.

My father is a few doors down playing horseshoes, well they are attempting to play. One guy sent the shoe soaring through the air and it landed on a car windshield, shattering the glass. That caused one of the many fights of the night.

The crowd of people around the *unofficial* horseshoe pit is the distraction I need.

Once I'm in the house, I haul ass to my room and grab both duffle bags, then hightail it out our back door.

Cutting across the yard, I run until I hit the fence that separates our yard from the back neighbors. I know they're at the party; I kept my eye on them.

Quickly I toss my bags over, then climb the four-foot chain link with ease.

I keep to the fence, not wanting to set off the motion security light they have as I make my way to the front.

Almost there.

Once on the street, I head right. There are very few streetlights that work, which is why I chose this road.

Up ahead, I can see Mitch's car. I run towards it.

Swinging open the passenger door, I toss my bags in the back, then I get in and shut the door… shut it on my past.

"Tori, where are you going?"

Mitch questions me as we pull into the bus station.

"I can't tell you. I'm sorry Mitch, but this is something I need to do on my own."

"Look, I get it. Your dad is an asshole, I don't blame you for leaving. But…" he parks the car and turns towards me. "Tori, I care about you. I mean, I don't think of you as just a piece of ass."

"Charming," I smile and punch him playfully in the arm. "I know you care and I do too. You're the only one who's ever been there for me. But it's better that you know nothing. Trust me."

He sighs and turns away from me.

"Promise me you'll call when you get wherever it is you're going."

There's sadness in his voice. I know I'll never call, but I can't tell him that. So I lie.

"I promise."

CHAPTER FOUR

TORI - AKA AMBER
16 YEARS OLD – A FRESH START

The bus trip was long and uncomfortable, but when I take that first step out onto the concrete pavement, a feeling of relief rushes over me.

Freedom!

I don't know where I'm going from here, but I don't care. Vegas is a big city with so much to offer.

A new beginning. A new life. A new me.

A taxi isn't hard to find. What is hard is telling the driver where to take me.

I ask him if he could recommend a cheap but decent hotel near the strip.

I assume he gets that question often because he hands me a pamphlet with many options for me to choose from.

My room isn't luxurious, but I have a bed and a bathroom. Oh, and a mini-fridge. Not bad for forty bucks a night.

I must find a job… fast. Even with a cheap motel and I still need to eat, eight hundred bucks won't last long.

After unpacking what little belongings I have, I head out to grab some food and drinks for my little fridge and get a few tourist booklets, hoping to find places to look for work. I plan to stay in tonight, make a list of jobs, and get a good night's sleep.

One thing I was smart about was using a different name when I had Donny make my fake ID. Wanting something simple, but believable, I went with Amber Clark.

There's just one problem… every place I've gone to wants a social security number, and I can't give that without giving myself up. I still have my real driver's license, but using that isn't an option… I won't go back to my father.

It's been two weeks since I arrived in Vegas. Still, no job and I have a hundred bucks left to my name.

I walked the streets for hours, I'm exhausted. It'll be dark soon and I learned shortly after arriving that the part of the city where my motel is, isn't all that great… especially for a girl wandering around the streets alone.

I make sure I'm back and in my room before the sun sets.

"Hey, Amber."

Tucker, the guy who works the night shift, stops me as I pass the counter.

"Hi, Tucker."

I've talked to him a few times, only when he strikes up a conversation, which I always try to cut short.

He's a nice guy, late twenties I'm guessing. His hair is long and straggly, always in his eyes.

"My friends and I are having a little party tomorrow night. Why don't you come? Don't you get bored sitting in that room all night?"

"I can't afford to do anything but sit in my room."

I don't know what made me tell him that, and my mouth decided it wasn't finished.

"I'll be leaving here tomorrow. I can't afford to stay."

"Did you lose your job?"

"What job?"

"Wait, where do you go all day?"

I sigh, my mouth has already started, I won't be around after tomorrow, no reason to stop now.

"I've been trying to find work, but…" I stop not knowing how much I should tell him.

"Are you in some sort of trouble?" he asks.

"It's complicated," what am I supposed to say? I'm a sixteen-year-old runaway with a fake ID that needs a job paying under the table?

I don't think so. I don't know him, and telling the wrong person is a one-way ticket back to my father.

"Listen, Amber, if you need help, if you are running from something or someone, you can trust me. Maybe there's something I can do."

Can I trust him?

"Tucker, it's complicated. I need a job, but I also need to stay low and off the radar."

"Tell you what, come to the party with me tomorrow night and I'll introduce you to a few friends that can most likely help you out with a job."

Most likely… that's the closest I've come to a job in my two weeks of searching.

"Fine, I'll go."

"Great, I'm off tomorrow but I'll swing by and pick you up around eight."

CHAPTER FIVE

TORI – AKA AMBER
16 YEARS OLD

The party isn't what I was expecting. Yes, there's music and drinking… but the men are mostly middle-aged. The women, I don't think one of them is older than twenty, hell a few could be my age… my real age.

Most of the women are topless, some bottomless.

"Tucker, these people are your friends?"

"Damn straight they are and nobody throws a party like Alec does. Go mingle, no one will bite you. I'll go grab us a drink."

Tucker walks away, leaving me standing in the middle of a room full of strangers.

Slowly, I back my way into the corner of the large open room.

This looks like the party I've seen a hundred times at my father's, but it feels different. None of these people give off a creepy vibe.

Yes, there are some naked. Yes, I see drugs on the table. But these people seem… happy. Not drunk happy or high on drugs happy. It's normal happy.

I'm reminded of the times I'd sit in the back of the lunchroom at school. I'd watch as groups of kids laughed and joked with one another. It always made me feel a bit of jealousy… just once I wanted to be normal. To be happy.

"Well, hey there sweet thing."

A tall brunette who is stunning walks up to me. Her southern accent tells me she's not from Vegas. She has on a tight pair of jean shorts that barely cover her ass, she's topless and I'm jealous of how perfect her tits are. And fuck me! The heels she's wearing… my God, they look fabulous on her, with her long, never-ending legs.

"I've never seen you here before."

"I'm here with Tucker."

"That man knows how to pick em'. You're a pretty little thing."

"Carmen, don't you have work to do?"

I look up to find a giant of a man standing next to Tucker.

My first instinct is to run, but my feet are frozen where I stand.

I have to strain my neck just to look at his face.

Holy Shit! This man is a God. A perfect face. He has a slight five-o'clock shadow, amazing but fierce green eyes, and his blonde hair is cut short on the sides and left longer on top with a messy look. His body is pure muscle from head to toe… in fact, he probably has more muscle in his little toe than I have on my entire body.

He's beautiful and terrifying at the same time.

Most people would tell me I'm too young to know anything about a man. But, growing up in my house, I've seen more than most forty-year-olds have.

"Amber, this is Alec," Tucker introduces.

"Hi, Alec," I stick my hand out expecting him to do the same but he just stares down at me.

"How old are you?" those green eyes look deep into mine like he's trying to read my mind.

"I'm... um... twenty-one."

He raises one eyebrow and I silently pray he can't read minds.

"You can go now Tucker," he says never taking his eyes off of me.

Tucker gives me a wink and turns to join the rest of the party.

All my senses tell me to go with him, but then Alec's hand takes my arm.

"Come on, let's go somewhere quiet to talk."

Alec runs an escort service. He's thirty-two years old, single, and offered me a job. Not as an escort, but as his secretary. Answering phones, setting appointments for the girls and guys. Pretty much anything he needs me to do.
I told him no at first and gave him no explanation when he asked why.

"Is it because you're running from something?" his question caught me off guard.

"Tucker tells me everything he knows about someone before bringing them here," he explains.

I confirmed what he already knew, but gave no specific details.

He told me I had nothing to worry about, he would pay me cash and no one else would know.

With that, I excepted his offer. We returned to the party, and he introduced me to a few of the girls, including Carmen, the southern beauty I met earlier.

And now here I am talking with Carmen, drinking some fruity concoction she made and smiling because I have a job and a new life to begin.

CHAPTER SIX

TORI – AKA AMBER
16 YEARS OLD

Tucker brought me back to the motel around three a.m.. Between exhaustion and those fruity drinks, Carmen kept making I slept like a rock until mid-afternoon.

After running to get food, I spent the rest of the weekend in my room.

Today is my first day of work. Thankfully Tucker offered to pick me up, saving me cab fare that I can't afford right now.

Alec assigned Carmen to teach me the ropes.

I had to take notes. Some girls would only see men, some only women, while most were ok with both.

There are three men and they all go both ways. That was easy to remember.

"You'll catch on quick," Carmen tells me. "Besides, most of the clients are regulars and tell you who they want to see. If you get a new client, they go straight to Alec. Anyone new has to go through an interview."

"How long have you been here?" I ask her.

"I've been with Alec for a year, before that I was a stripper."

"Is it… weird? I mean uncomfortable being with people you don't know?"

"It's not all about sex, I have a couple of guys that only want a dinner companion and some conversation."

"Really?"

"Hey, if some guy wants to pay four hundred bucks to take me to dinner… who am I to complain?"

"Four hundred?"

"Well, Alec gets some, but the tips we get are one hundred percent ours to keep."

My head spins with possibilities.

"How do you become one of Alec's girls?"

"Sweetie, let me tell you a little secret… you're already one of Alec's girls."

The days went by fast. One week turned into two… two into three, and before I knew it a month had flown by.

Everyone was sweet to me, especially Alec.

I'd saved up enough money to get my own apartment, but I needed to save more.

The lady who owned the building I looked at wanted first and last month's rent, plus a security deposit.

I didn't realize how expensive things would be and that would've let me broke… again.

I started dropping hints to Alec that I wanted to do what the other girls did.

He would act like he didn't hear me and talk about something else… until today.

"Why?" he asks.

"Why what?" I'm confused by his question.

"Tell me why you want to be like the other girls?"

"For one, it's better money. Two, I don't want to live in a crummy motel anymore. And three, I'm old enough to make my own decisions."

"Are you really twenty-one?"

"Yes! For the hundredth time."

"Are you in trouble with the law? Is that what you're running from?"

"What! No! I've never been in trouble like that."

"Ok, I'll give you a trial run. If, after a couple of times out there, you still want to do it, then I will put you full-time with the other girls. And you can move into one of my apartments."

"You have apartments?"

"Several. Now go find Carmen, tell her to take you shopping. Jeans and T-shirts won't cut it if you want to be one of the girls."

"You look like you're ready to lose your lunch," Carmen says as she straightens my hair.

"I'm a little nervous. This isn't like going on a date."

"No, it's better. You get paid."

I won't have to do this forever. I tell myself. I'll save every penny and get out on my own.

"Here, take this."

Carmen hands me a white pill.

"What is it?"

"Just something to calm your nerves. It won't hurt you." I pop the pill in my mouth and take a drink of water. "Time to go sweet thing," she pulls me out of the chair and gives my ass a smack before pushing me towards the door.

Phillip, if that's his real name, dropped me off at my motel around midnight.

I was planning to go back to Alec's after my *date,* but whatever that pill was, it definitely relaxed me and now I'm sleepy.

I change out of the little black dress Carmen made me buy and go to slip into something more comfortable, my cotton shorts and a tank top, but not before showering.

I grab my purse and crawl into bed, stacking the pillows so I can sit up.

Reaching my hand in my purse, I pull out a wad of cash.

My lips turn up into a smile and I make a mental note to get some pills from Carmen.

I will need them.

I won't have to do this forever, but…

I can do this!

CHAPTER SEVEN

TORI – 18 YEARS OLD
TWO YEARS LATER

The ice pack on my cheek does nothing to relieve the sting.

I pissed Alec off again.

"You need to stop this Amber."

I roll my eyes at Carmen and take the joint from her hand.

"There's nothing wrong with me making a little side money."

"By the looks of the bruise on your cheek, Alec thinks differently."

"He'll get over it, he always does."

I take a long hit from the joint, holding it in and calming myself before exhaling.

I've been seeing clients on the side. I'm usually careful of when and where it happens, but Alec gets suspicious and I get greedy, which lowers my guard and I get caught.

The first time he caught me, he beat the shit out of the client and banned him from ever using the service again.

The second time, I stepped in the way and sported a black eye for about a week.

He warned me to stop, but I ignored his warning and got smarter about how I did things.

No more seeing clients from the service on the side. I found my own, or they found me.

One being a married couple.

I met them while having dinner with a client. I was in the ladies' room when I was approached by the wife.

She and her husband were friends with Phillip, who was the first man Alec sent me out to.

Phillip has a bondage kink, and I found out I enjoyed being tied up.

The woman's husband was into bondage, but also whips, crops, and other things. Things his wife did not like and refused to take part in.

That's where I came in, recommended by Phillip.

The arrangement is… the husband can use all his kinks on me, but he's not allowed to fuck me with his cock, that is only for his wife. His wife and I are allowed to play with each other, and that's usually at the end when he's ready to fuck her while watching us.

We meet once a month, on one of my days off and only at their house. They live outside of Vegas and the cab fare isn't cheap, but they pay for it and give me five hundred dollars for two hours of my time.

That money gets stashed away, far from Alec. I will use that money to get out on my own.

It's Friday night and all us girls are getting ready to head out. The weekends are always booked with clients and unless you are deathly ill, you're going out. Alec gives no one a break on the weekend.

Tonight I've got a well-known high roller that spends every weekend at the casinos. I'm to meet him there, in the lounge.

I've never been with the guy, but the girls told me all about him.

Have a few drinks in the lounge, be his arm candy at the tables, then up to his room.

"Hopefully you're his good luck charm," Carmen tells me. "I've heard he gives a hefty tip if he's winning."

"Here's to good luck," I raise my shot glass full of whiskey in the air before downing it.

I arrived at the hotel about fifteen minutes early. I scan the room as I make my way to the VIP section.

A tall man wearing a black suit stands next to the door.

"Hi, I'm Amber Clark. I'm meeting Mr. Bison."

"Yes, Ms. Clark, follow me, please."

He leads me into the VIP section. There are several groups of men and women. Some dressed in tuxes and evening gowns, others in casual dress slacks and shirt or cocktail dresses.

I'm glad I chose a dress that fits in.

Black silk, a strap over one shoulder, leaving the other one bare. The neckline comes down at an angle, and the back is open to the bottom of my waist. The fabric flows down to just above my knees. It's just tight enough to show off my curves, but not too tight that it clings to my body. I left my legs nude to show off my tan, and I'm wearing a pair of four-inch heels that have a silk ribbon that wraps around my ankle.

I'm led to the far corner. Three men sit in a booth. All three of them panty-melting hot and all three staring at me when we approach the table.

"Mr. Bison, your guest, Ms. Clark."

The man at the end closest to me stands.

He's around six-foot, thick jet black hair that's perfectly combed. His eyes are almost as dark as his hair. The white dress shirt he's wearing fits snug to his chest, the sleeves uncuffed and rolled, it shows he's fit but it's just a tease to what muscle I imagine lies beneath.

"Thank you, Charles," his voice is deep and powerful. He slips a bill into the man's hand and then turns to me.

"Ms. Clark, please have a seat," he steps aside and I slide into the booth. "Can I pour you a drink or would you prefer a glass of wine?"

I look at the bottle on the table. *Bulleit.* A whiskey I've never heard of.

"I'll have what you're drinking, please."

He pours me a glass. I know little about fancy expensive alcohol but I know if it's not in a shot glass you probably shouldn't down it in one go.

He slides the glass to me, and I take a small sip. It's smooth, and the warmth of it relaxes me as it glides down my throat.

After a few drinks, Andre and I head over to a Blackjack table. His friends Seth and Evan join us.

"A kiss for good luck?" Andre puts a chip to my lips once again, this time it's a five-thousand-dollar chip. I press my lips to it and graze the tip of his finger and slide my tongue over it before pulling back. He takes the chip and places it on top of another chip.

Andre has had me kiss the chips each time, some hands won, but most have not.

The dealer throws the first card out. My knees go weak when I see the Ace of Hearts.   I know little about gambling, but I know an Ace can be very good. When the next card is dealt time stops… A King of Spades… Twenty-one! Blackjack!

After a few more hands, Andre collects his winnings and tells me he'd like to have another drink before heading to his room. Again Seth and Evan join us.

"Where are you from, Amber?'
"San Diego," I lie to Andre. I wasn't expecting personal questions. I figured drinks,

gambling, and sex. But I've been here for four hours and we haven't left the main floor.

"How long have you been with Alec?"

"About two years."

I feel his hand slip under my dress and move up to my inner thigh. I suck in a breath when his finger traces over my panties and presses down on my clit. He lowers his mouth to my ear.

"Amber, how do you feel about sharing?" his finger presses harder, and he circles over my sensitive nub. "You see my friends here would like to make an appointment with you," his circles increase. "But, I say, why wait?"

My thighs tighten around his hand and at that same moment, I feel another hand run up my other leg.

I turn my head to see Seth has moved closer.

Seth pulls my legs apart then pulls my panties to the side allowing Andre's finger to slip through my folds and then places his finger on my clit.

"This would be between the four of us. No need to involve Alec," Andre informs me.

"Ok," Is all I'm able to get out because he pushes his finger deeper into my pussy, his finger crooking up and rolling around hitting just the right spot that sends me over the edge, losing myself to erotic orgasm right here in a lounge full of strangers.

CHAPTER EIGHT

TORI - AKA AMBER
18 YEARS OLD

Andre's room is a VIP, and it's bigger than my apartment, hell, the living room alone is bigger than my apartment.

There is a kitchen and a fully stocked bar. But what catches my eye is the glass wall that opens up to a balcony that overlooks the strip. I walk over to it; the view is amazing.

I see Andre's reflection in the glass; he comes up behind me. His hands run down my body to the hem of my dress. He makes his way back up, bringing the silky material with him.

I watch him in the glass, his dark eyes lift to meet mine. My body responds to his touch, his hands leave a trail of heat in their path.

He takes his time lifting the dress over my head and when I'm free of it, the cool air in the room mixes with the heat of his touch, making my body tremble.

"You are gorgeous," Andre says as he circles his fingertips over my nipples.

I see movement from the corner of my eye and look back up to the glass where I see Seth and Evan have joined us.

Three seductive men.

Three sets of hands explore my body.

Three pairs of lips press soft kisses over my tingling skin.

The feeling is sensual. It's filthy. It's erotic.

I place my hands on the glass window to steady myself. My eyes close and I focus on the feeling of their touch. I don't know who's doing what and I don't care.

My nipple is sucked into a mouth, teeth bite down.

"Mmm," I moan.

"That's it beautiful, feel it," I hear Andre's deep voice. "This is all about you. Feel it… feel us."

A finger slips into my pussy. A set of hands grip my ass cheeks. My breasts are being sucked by two mouths. Another mouth bites my ass as fingers knead my skin.

My body is having a sensation overload.

"God Damn, your pussy is soaked."

Andre is the one to speak again.

I open my eyes and see him lower down, his head going between my legs where his finger is teasing my pussy.

He spreads my legs further apart and runs his tongue over my clit before sucking it into his mouth. He bites down, a sting followed by a sharp pain sets my clit on fire. But then Andre massages my clit with his tongue and the pain turns into a pleasure unlike any I've felt before.

"Oh, fuck!" I cry out. My knees go weak.

"Hold on gorgeous, grab my shoulders."

My hands press hard, and my fingernails dig into his flesh.

His tongue doesn't stop and his fingers push deep into my pussy.

Just when I think I can't take anymore, another shot of pain hits. Teeth bite my ass cheeks and a finger slips into my tight puckered hole.

"Oh, God!"

My nipple is sucked harder before teeth latch on.

I explode. An orgasm so intense it feels as if my soul is being ripped from me.

Three seductive men.

Three sets of hands explored my body.

Their lips, tongues, and teeth sucked, licked, and marked my body into one soul-shattering orgasm.

I wake in the tight hold of Andre's arms.

Slowly, I slip out of his embrace.

The clock on the nightstand shows six-fifteen am.

Shit! Alec will have my ass for this.

I go into the bathroom to freshen up. Looking at my body in the mirror, I see red marks and bruises from my breasts down to my thighs.

An image of last night flashes in my head. Phantom pain tingles across my skin. I've felt pain many times in my life at the hands of my father, his friends, and Alec. But the pain I received from Andre, Seth, and Evan took away the bad pain. It made me forget, yet it also reminded me I'm a survivor. I can't explain how one pain can hurt so bad while another pain can feel so good and make me feel alive. It's an explanation I don't have but, I can tell you… I want more.

CHAPTER NINE

TORI – AKA AMBER
18 YEARS OLD

I had the taxi drop me off down the road from the apartment building. Alec will be pissed if he knows I stayed out all night.

I make it to my door without running into anyone. I don't have to worry about making noise with keys because none of our doors have locks.

When Alec told me I could move into one of his apartments, I pictured… well, an apartment.

What he owns is a two-story building that he transformed into a living space. There are eight suites, each with a bedroom, bathroom, a small living room, and a kitchen… if you can call it that with its 2 burner stove, and a fridge that doesn't hold much. Downstairs is like a house that is for his use only.

I sigh in relief when I reach my bedroom. I'm tired and sore. I hang my dress up and put on a pair of yoga pants and a tank top, then slip under the covers to get a couple more hours of sleep.

"What the fuck!" I'm jolted awake. Pain burns my scalp, I'm being dragged out of bed by my hair. My knees crash to the floor.

"Where the fuck was you all night?"

Alec yanks my head back. His face is red, his eyes are full of rage.

"Fucking answer me!" he pulls me to my feet by my hair.

"Alec, please. Stop."

His other hand grips my jaw, his large hand is tight if he squeezes and harder he'd probably crush my bones.

"Did you stay all fucking night with Andre Bison?"

I can't tell him I did. I want to see Andre again… so I lie.

"N… No," it's hard to speak with his death grip. Tears fill my eyes from the pain.

Finally, he releases me, but shoves my head back forcing me to stumble, I lose my balance and fall to the floor.

"Get up!" he screams.

I scramble to my feet.

"Where the fuck were you then?"

Lie to him.

"I hooked up with a guy I met at the casino. I… I'm sorry, Alec."

He turns his head; I think he's going to walk away, but before I can move his hand flies back, connecting with the side of my face.

I crumble to the ground.

"You're a cunt and a whore and I fucking own you… and don't you fucking forget it"

He walks out the door and slams it shut.

Alec left me alone, and I slept… uncomfortably because of the pain throbbing in my head. Not even the pills Carmen gave me dulled the pain.

It's only four in the afternoon. I have three hours before I have to get dressed for my next appointment. I don't know how I will make it through tonight; I need something to take the edge off.

I don't want to leave my room in fear of seeing Alec, so I shoot Carmen a quick text.

Me: *Come over and bring your goodie bag.*
Carmen: *Be there in a few.*

I toss my phone on the table and go to the kitchen to make some coffee.

"Jesus girl, you look like shit."

Carmen plops her ass on the couch next to me and tosses a bag on the table.

"I feel worse than I look, trust me."

"You really had Alec in a fucking mood last night. What the fuck were you thinking, staying with that guy all night?"

I love Carmen, but the less she knows, the safer she is.

"I wasn't with him all night. I met a guy at the casino and hooked up with him after I finished with Andre."

"You have a death wish? You need to cut this shit out."

"Save the lecture, Carmen. Just give me something for the pain and roll me a joint for later."

An hour later I'm relaxed, and the pain has faded. I'm just about to get up and head to the shower when my door flies open and Alec storms in.

"Change of plans. I'm sending you out with Eva. Be ready in forty-five minutes." He turns and walks out, not bothering to shut the door.

Shit! Sending me out with Eva is his way of telling me he's keeping an eye on me.

Eva is his little pet. No secrets are safe with her. She tells Alec everything. which means he'll find out about all the marks on my body the second we get back tonight.

CHAPTER TEN

TORI – AKA AMBER
18 YEARS OLD

I had given up hope to ever seeing Andre again. A month had gone by and he never called to make an appointment with any of us girls.

It rekindled my hope today when Carmen told me he called and requested me for Friday night.

Two more days and Andre can feed me the pain I've been craving. I'll be able to replace the bad with the good.

The night Eva told Alec about the marks on my body, he went crazy. Told me I was a whore that liked it rough, then he showed me his version of rough.

A version that will be forever scarred on my skin.

Carmen did what she could to clean the wounds by changing the bandages and applying an ointment, but the cuts were deep and rough… just how Alec intended them to be.

It wasn't the same pain I felt with Andre, but my body responded to it and I got off and that pissed Alec off even more.

"Hey, your birthday is next week," Carmen says as she shoves a cream-filled donut in her mouth.

"Yes, it is."

I'll be nineteen, but I'm the only one here that knows, everyone thinks I'll be twenty-four.

In two weeks, the Fourth of July will be here marking my third year since I ran away from home. Shortly after that, it will be three years of me working for Alec. A plan I never intended to last this long.

"Let's go shopping tomorrow, buy yourself a new outfit for your night with Mr. Highroller."

It would be nice to get out. Over the past month, I've only gone to appointments and a few quick trips to the grocery store. I haven't even gone out with any of the men or women I see on the side. My body needed a rest from Alec's anger.

"That sounds fun. Let's go to lunch as well. I can use a day out."

"Sweet! Just the two of us, or do you want to see if anyone else is free?"

"No, just us."

"Ok, let's go to the Fashion Show."

"Alright, but I know you only want to go there because you love the Greek Restaurant."

"Best food in Vegas, if you ask me."

"Ok, Fashion Show and Greek food. Now, take your donuts and get out. I'm going to take a shower then go to bed."

Carmen shoves another donut in her mouth.

"I can't help it, the weed Tucker got me is the shit and all I crave are donuts. You want the rest of this joint for later?"

"No, I've had enough. You finish it."

She grabs the half-smoked joint and her box of donuts then leaves and I head for a long hot shower.

"Amber, you will look fucking hot tomorrow night."

I throw my bags on the bed and Carmen grabs the garment bag from my hand. She hangs it on the wall hook and unzips the bag, revealing the crimson red dress.

The front and back are cut into a thin narrow "V" both stopping at my waist. I made sure that the material wasn't to open in the back, I didn't want my scars to be showing. At least Alec was thoughtful enough to put them where they can be hidden. *Thoughtful fucking asshole.* From the waist down, the material fits my body perfectly and flows down to my feet, and there's a slit that goes up to my hip.

I bought a silver chain the hangs down between my breasts with earrings to match and to complete the outfit a pair of crimson and silver stilettos.

"I hope Andre wins big. This outfit cost me a small fortune, I will need a big tip."

"Shit, girl, when he sees you in this he will give you the money to buy one in every color," Carmen winks at me. "When he mentions the dress, tell him how stunning the emerald green one was."

"Should I also mention the four-hundred dollar price tag?"

"That's chump change to him, I'd tell him double."

"I was being sarcastic."

"Suit yourself. So what are we doing tonight?"

"Doesn't matter to me. You decide."

"I was hoping you'd say that. My appointment is with Stevie tomorrow."

"Oh, hell. I'm sorry."

Stevie is a regular client. He's a cute, rich, arrogant man with a matchstick for a dick. He always brings his condoms, I think he has them specially made to fit his tiny cock.

"So, we staying here or in my room tonight?"

"Let's stay here, I have a better mattress."

Carmen and I have an arrangement. Anytime one of us gets stuck with Stevie, we spend the night before getting each other off because lord knows it won't happen with Stevie. He doesn't notice that we are good at faking it.

"I'll go get my things, you order a pizza."

"Jesus, Carmen, how many toys are we going to need? And when did you buy more? This one is new."

"Oh, honey, wait until you feel that. Get up on the bed, I'll show you."

I slide my panties off and climb up on the mattress. I settle myself in the middle and use the pillow to prop my head up so I can watch Carmen.

"Spread em' open babe."

Carmen moves between my legs and places the vibrator on my stomach. Her head dips down, and her tongue pushes into my pussy.

"Fuck!" this girl can work a tongue better than most men can work a dick.

She slips a finger inside of me and her mouth sucks on my clit. My hands fist her hair and I pull her tighter to me.

"Bite me," I scream out to her. "Bite my fucking clit."

She sucks my clit between her teeth and bites down.

"Ah, fuck!" my entire body shakes and I explode like a fucking geyser.

"Holy shit, that was one hell of an orgasm." Carmen licks around her shiny wet lips. "You need to do that to me… multiple times."

She tosses the vibrator off my stomach and crawls up to me, her lips press to mine.

"Mmm," I moan out from the taste of me on her lips. "I'm going to make you come so God

Damn hard you'll still be feeling it tomorrow night when Stevie puts his tiny dick in you."

CHAPTER ELEVEN

TORI – AKA AMBER
18 YEARS OLD

It's just Andre and me tonight. I had expected Seth and Evan to be sitting at the table when I arrived.

We had a couple of drinks, played a few hands of Blackjack, and now we are up in his room, the same one from the last time I was here.

"I ordered us some dinner," he says as he hands me a glass of wine.

"Oh, ok," I'm surprised. I wasn't expecting to have dinner with him.

"Finish your wine, then take your clothes off, but leave the heels on."

"Shouldn't I wait until after they bring the food?"

"No, I want you naked and sitting at the table when it arrives."

My stomach flutters and my hand shakes as I attempt to bring the glass to my lips, once there I don't pull it away until the glass in empty.

I slip out of my dress and take off my panties, leaving my heels on as told.

Andre pulls out the chair at the end of the table that faces the door. I sit down and as if on cue, there's a knock on the door. He opens it, standing where my view is blocked.

"Bring it to the table." He says and steps aside.

A tall, skinny guy who looks to be maybe in his early twenties pushes a cart into the room. His eyes land on me just as Andre shuts the door, leaving no quick escape for the man who looks like a deer caught in headlights.

"Don't be shy," Andre says and pushes him along towards the table.

The man's eyes look away, but I can see them darting around the room, looking for something… anything else to focus on besides me.

Andre comes and stands behind me, his hands trail over my shoulders down to my breasts.

"She's beautiful. Isn't she?" he asks the nervous man as he puts our plates on the table with shaking hands. "A woman this beautiful needs to be shown off." He pinches my nipples, causing me to gasp. "Wouldn't you agree?"

The man nods his head, unable to speak.

Andre laughs and moves over to him.

"Leave the rest of the food on the cart," he reaches in his pocket and pulls out a couple of bills, handing it to the man. "That'll be all for the night," he dismisses him.

After we finished our meal, Andre put the plates on the cart and moved it outside the door.

"I bought you a present," he picks up a long black box with a silver ribbon tied around it and brings it over to me.

I undo the ribbon and remove the lid. A silver chain lays in the box. A necklace… or so I thought. When I pull out the velvet insert, I reveal a set of nipple clamps attached to the ends of the chain.

"As I recall, you loved having your nipples bitten," he takes the chain from me and attaches the clips to my nipples. "And seeing that I have other plans with my mouth and your body I thought these would be fitting."

I suck in a breath from the tightness.

"You like that?"

"Y-Yes," I say breathlessly.

"Good, because I have more presents in the bedroom."

He takes my hand and leads me to the bedroom. There's a case on the floor next to the bed.

"Go lay down in the center of the mattress. Arms above your head, legs apart, and keep the heels on."

I do as I'm told.

Click, click.

I hear Andre free the latches on the case. Even when I lift my head, I still can't see what's in it. When he stands, he is holding a long piece of silk, which he places over my eyes and ties it snug behind my head.

He must be back in the case, I can hear things moving around.

I've been blindfolded before, but I've always known what would happen.

I don't know what Andre has in that case or what he will do to me, and the anticipation makes my pulse quicken.

Silence. The noise from the case stops. I listen for movement, but there is none.

I focus, listening for the sound of his breathing.

Nothing.

Silence.

Did he leave?

The anticipation heightens and mixes with a hint of fear.

I raise my head and move my hands to untie the blindfold.

Smack!

"Oh, God!"

Pain, pleasure, and excitement hit me all at once. It feels as if a thousand blades bit into my skin. It's a flogger, leather… I think. And he struck me across my clamped breasts.

Silence again.

I don't move.

Smack!

Across one thigh, the ends of the tassels nip over my clit. My back arches off the bed.

Smack! Smack! Smack!

Thigh! Breasts! Thigh!

My nipples and clit are on fire. It's intense and I want more.

Silence again… except for my heavy breathing and rapid heartbeat.

I know Andre is near me. I can feel his presence. I take a calming breath. With not being able to see, I let my other senses take control.

My ears pick up the faint, soft sound of movement to my left. Then I feel him, his hand takes my wrist, something silky wraps around and when he pulls it, my arm rises and stays in place. He does the same with my other arm.

I'm tied to the bed.

I feel his breath near my mouth; he doesn't kiss me, instead, he lightly runs his tongue over my lips.

"I knew you would look amazing tied to my bed."

His deep voice sends a chill down my spine.

He runs his hand down between my breasts. The feeling is rough but gentle. Something is covering his hand.

When he reaches my clit, his touch is light and soothing. Then with a quick movement, he raises his hand from me and brings it back down quickly and hard.

"Oh, God!"

A stinging pleasure races through me.

"Do you like that?" he asks and returns to a soothing touch.

"More, please," I beg.

I hear his chuckle before he moves his hand up and back down… even harder than before.

"Yes! Again!" I scream.

Pain… pleasure… pain… pleasure. My body hums from the sensation overload.

Again and again. Over and over. Until I can't take it anymore and an orgasm rips through me, and right at the peak of my explosion Andre lifts my legs throwing them over his shoulders and slams his cock deep into my pussy.

"Fuck! You are so tight," he growls out.

I try to scream out, but I've lost the ability to speak. The cry of pleasure locked inside my head cause my ears to ring.

I'm fucked into an orgasm so intense it feels as if my body has been sucked into a black hole. Thrown into oblivion. Unaware of everything except the feeling of pure fucking ecstasy.

Andre ran us a bath. I relaxed, and he gently washed my body. Afterward, he rubbed me down with creams and oils, giving extra care to all my red swollen spots.

"What are these scars from?" he asks me as his hand's massage cream into my back.

"I had an accident," I lie out loud while the voice in my head screams *My Father and Alec.*

"What kind of accident?"

"I'd rather not talk about it. I need to get going it's late."

"You're staying with me this weekend. I have a friend coming into the city tomorrow, I want you to meet him."

"I can't. I have to be back tonight."

"Says who?"

"Alec."

"I'll handle him."

He gets off the bed and grabs his phone.

"Andre, no. Please."

He ignores my plea.

"Alec it's Andre. Amber is staying with me for the weekend."

I don't need to hear what Alec's response is, the rage in Andre's voice tells me what I already knew he would say.

"I don't fucking care what your rules are. I bring you more business than you deserve and I can take it all away!"

Oh, God. I will pay for this.

"Smart decision, not that you had a choice. She'll be back on Sunday."

Andre tosses his phone on the dresser.

"All settled. You're staying."

CHAPTER TWELVE

Andre's friend Demetri showed up Saturday evening just before dinner.

He's slightly taller than Andre, with a rock-solid body full of muscle. He has the same jet black hair, but longer. The resemblance is so striking, you would think they were related. And just like Andre, he knew how to play in the bedroom.

I expected to find myself covered in bruises when I looked in the mirror, but I found none. I had redness and markings, even a few welts. My nipples are sore and red, my clit is swollen, and my pussy and ass are not only red and swollen... they are raw.

Both Andre and Demetri were careful, I had a safe word, and they slowly increased each strike, waiting for me to break down and cry out my word. What they didn't know is my tolerance for pain is off the charts when it comes to pleasure.

What Andre and Demetri gave me, my body absorbed it. The higher the pain, the more intense the pleasure was.

When I woke this morning, neither Andre nor Demetri was in the suite.

I take a quick shower and put my dress on. Had I known I'd be staying, I would have brought another outfit.

I find a tray on the dining table with two carafes. One coffee, one orange juice, along with muffins and a bowl of fruit.

I don't know where Andre has gone or when he'll return, so I help myself and wait.

Halfway through my bowl of fruit, Andre returns… alone.

"I see you found the breakfast I had ordered for you."

"Yes, thank you."

"I'll be checking out soon, I'll drive you home."

"No, that's ok. I can call for a taxi."

"I wasn't asking, Amber. I will drive you home."

An hour later, Andre is pulling up to my apartment building.

I open the door to get out, but Andre stops me.

"Don't forget these," he hands me the box with the nipple clamps. "Bring them with you next weekend," he kisses me. "This is for you from Demetri. I'll see you soon."

Before I step into the building, I shove the envelope from Demetri into my purse.

Everything is quiet when I walk in. I rush up the stairs to my apartment. I open the door and jump back.

"Alec! You scared me."

He looks pissed.

"Come here," he pats the cushion on the couch.

"I'm tired, Alec. Can we…"

"Get the fuck over here. Right. Now. Tori!"

I gasp when he says my name… my real name.

Instinct and fear tell me to run… and I do, but Alec catches me just before I make it to my bedroom.

I panic when he shoves me in my room. The contents of my closet are tossed all over the floor, except for my little box. The one that holds my past.

"You lying little bitch," he throws me to the ground. His foot connects with my ribs, knocking the air from my lungs.

"A-Alec, please…"

"Shut your fucking mouth and get up!" he pulls a fist full of my hair yanking me up.

The pain in my ribs causing me to scream. I try to hold my side, but the sudden impact of Alec's fist sends me back to the ground.

"Eighteen! You're only eighteen fucking years old! I bet mommy and daddy would love to know what their slut of a daughter has been doing."

"No! Please," I beg.

"You're a fucking runaway. Well, guess what sweetheart, you ran the wrong way and straight into a nightmare that is me. What did I tell you before?"

He drags me to my feet and slams me against the wall. His fingers dig into my face.

"Do you remember what I said?"

I shake my head.

"Well then, let me refresh your memory. You're a cunt and a whore, and I fucking own you!" his face moves close to mine as he forces my head to turn to the side, his mouth close to my ear. "That's if you want to keep your secret," he pulls back and lands another fist to my ribs. "I'll be holding on to this," he flashes the piece of plastic with my true identity in front of my eyes. "Don't fucking test me, bitch!"

When he leaves my room, I collapse to the floor.

I can't have my father knowing where I am. It doesn't matter that I'm no longer sixteen. He's a monster, one worse than Alec. If he knew where I was, he'd find a way to get me back into his grip and there would be no escape.

Alec is right… he fucking owns me.

CHAPTER THIRTEEN

TORI
TWENTY-TWO YEARS OLD

"Carmen don't be so fucking greedy."

She wets her finger and dips it in the white powder before running it over my lips.

"We have plenty, Am-ori."

"Stop calling me that."

After Alec discovered my lie and beat the hell out of me, I told Carmen my secret. I knew she would keep it to herself. It pissed her off that I kept it from her, but she got over it by annoying me with her little nickname for me *Am-ori* a combination of Amber and Tori.

"Never," she laughs. "Besides, it sounds sexy."

"You're such a goof. What time do you have to head out?"

"Around seven. I'm meeting Mr. Swings Left."

We have nicknames for some of the men. Like Mr. Swings Left, he got his name because of his dick; it curves to the left, and not just slightly… any further and his name would have been Mr. U Turn.

"I'm staying in. When you're finished tonight, come back to my room."

Bad night for me to stay in. I'm coked up and can't sit still.

I'm not a drug addict, I use occasionally to help me through the day. There are days I'm so tired I need the pick me up, so I do a few lines. There are other days I just need to mellow out, so I smoke a joint or two. Sometimes it's pills because my body is beaten and bruised.

I've become braver over the years with Alec, but I still haven't found the courage to leave.

I had stopped all side work with people right after Alec found out my secret. Things calmed down, except for when Andre was in town.

Alec has a love/hate thing going on. He loves Andre's money, but hates Andre, even more so since he refused to see anyone but me... until I ruined it.

I found out how much I love pain. Not the pain you get from having the shit kicked out of you, no, the pain that I love enhances my sexual pleasure.

I pushed myself further and further. I'd spend hours online researching. Then I started pushing Andre. He was game for most, but even with his love of marking me, he told me my need... my obsession with pain was too much.

It's been over a year since I've seen him. I know he's still around; I hear the other girls talk about him.

I've had clients that will use a crop or a paddle on me, but none were man enough to use them the way I wanted.

Carmen thinks I'm crazy. I even tried to get her to push the limits. She cried and told me I'm seeking abuse. She didn't understand. For me, it's a pleasure that makes me forget the abuse. It's a pleasure of pain that I can control and reminds me I'm a survivor.

It's been weeks since I've had anyone come close to satisfying me.

The pain I seek has suppressed my nightmares over the years, but now they have returned and I drown myself in a bottle more and more each day.

I need relief. I need to forget.

My decision comes easily. After my appointment tonight, I will find what I need. Damn the consequences of Alec. Damn everyone who doesn't understand.

My appointment didn't last very long. The client was a first-timer. A recently divorced guy in his mid-forties who has never been with any woman other than his ex-wife.

His business partner is a frequent client and talked him into tonight. Pairing him with me wasn't a good thing. I swear I thought the man was going to lose his nut just from me slipping a condom on his cock.

I head over to the neighborhood where I first lived. It's not the greatest, but chances are I'll find what I'm looking for.

It's Saturday night, the streets are crowded and I head to the one bar I know gets a lot of action.

I find a seat at the far end of the bar, a perfect place to scope everyone out.

"What can I get you?" the bartender slaps the counter in front of me.

"A seven and seven please, with two limes on the side."

"Can I see your ID?"

I pull my wallet out and slide my ID to him.

"One seven and seven coming up."

"With two limes," I remind him.

My eyes scan the room and stop on a man standing by the pool table. Tall and muscular. He's wearing blue jeans and a tight black t-shirt. His arms are covered in tattoos and I can see ink peeking out above the collar. His blonde hair is cut short on the sides, the top is long and pulled back in a tie.

He's gorgeous and my target.

I pick up my drink and walk over to the pool table. It doesn't take long for his eyes to find me.

"Mind if I play?" I ask him and take a sip of my drink, my eyes never leaving his.

"We're playing for cash, little girl. Fifty bucks a game."

I reach into my purse, pull out a hundred and throw it on the table.

"Don't bother getting me change, I won't need it," I take the stick from his hands. "Ladies first."

One hour, three-seven and seven, and one beer later, I ran the table not once, but twice.

"Are you a hustler?"

Rod asks me or as I like to call him Sir Flex-a-lot. This guy flexes his muscles every chance he gets.

"No, not a hustler. My father had a pool table, and I used to play for hours when I was growing up."

He pulls me by my waist towards him. "So what do we do now?"

"You got a place close by?"

"I'm staying at a motel down the road."

"Good, let's go."

It's a short walk to his place. The room isn't much, but it's enough for what I need.

"I have some rules," I tell Rod as he twists the cap off two bottles of beer.

"What kind of rules?"

"First - you wear a condom. Second - no oral, we don't know one another, so oral is off the table, the same goes for kissing. And the last rule… I like it rough."

"Rough?" he raises an eyebrow and steps closer to me. "So, if I do this," his hand goes around my throat and his mouth lowers to my tits and he bites down, his teeth grabbing my nipple through my clothing and he lets go too quickly. I sigh when he releases my throat.

"Is that too rough?"

"No."

"Take your clothes off."

We both strip down. His cock isn't impressively long, but he's thick.

I pull a few condoms out of my purse.

"If you plan on fucking my ass, you will put a new condom on before you put your dick back into my pussy."

"Baby, I hope you have more condoms because I will have that sweet ass more than once."

I pull out the last two condoms and toss them with the others. He grabs one and slides it over his cock.

Rod spins me around and bends me over the edge of the bed.

Smack!

His hand connects with my ass.

"Yes!" I cry out.

He smacks me again.

"Fuck! Harder!"

Rod doesn't hesitate and gives me three hard blows in a row.

"Damn, girl. That's fucking hot."

He flips me over and spreads my legs wide. One hand moves to my throat and the other lines his cock up with my pussy.

"If I get to rough..."

"Just fuck me already!" I scream.

He grips my throat and slams into me at the same time.

"More," I grunt out.

His cock pumps harder and his mouth finds my tit once again and he bites, sucks, and licks, switching back and forth between each breast.

This feels great, but I need more.

CHAPTER FOURTEEN

TORI
TWENTY-TWO YEARS OLD

Rod found his way and got creative to give me the fix I needed, including using one of the empty beer bottles. Not one of my proudest moments, but I got off on the pain. It was a new kind of high.

We may have gotten carried away, but I don't care.

I leave Rod sleeping and walk back down to the bar where I know taxis are hanging around.

"Amber"

Someone yells out my name, I turn around.

Fuck!

"Tucker, what are you doing here?"

"I work down the street. Did you forget? What are you doing here? Better yet, what the fuck happened to you?"

He reaches for my neck. I back away.

"It's nothing. I got to go, Tucker. I'll talk to you later."

I turn and walk fast, lucky to find a taxi sitting just up ahead. I jump in the back and give the driver my address.

A loud bang jolts me awake. The covers are pulled off of me.

"Didn't I fucking warn you?"

I'm dragged out of bed and into the bathroom.

My eyes close from the sudden brightness.

"You're not a very smart bitch. I have eyes all over this city… especially on you."

Alec faces me towards the mirror.

The tank top and shorts I have on display all the marks and bruises I have.

"You've had your last warning, I told you I fucking own you." He drags me back to the bed. "I tell you who you can and can't fuck. I control the cock that goes inside your cunt."

I see him reach for the buckle on his belt. What happens next happens so fast I can't stop myself.

My hand grabs the lamp off the nightstand and I swing hard, cracking the side of Alec's head.

The adrenaline pumping through me feels like an electric current.

I hit him again.

"You don't fuckin' own me," I push hard and he stumbles back. Blood runs down the side of his face. I take advantage and rip the cord of the lamp from the wall so I can move towards him.

"I'm not a scared sixteen-year-old girl anymore," I swing hard, connecting with his jaw. "And I'm done being afraid of you and your threats. Do you hear me, Alec? I'm. Fucking. Done!" I raise my arm and with everything I have I land one more blow to his head and for the first time, he is the one crumbling to the ground.

I don't know if he's knocked out or if he's dead, and I don't fucking care. For the first time in a long time, I feel free.

I rush to my closet and throw some clothes in a bag.

"Am-ori! What the fuck happened?"

Carmen rushes over to Alec. She checks his pulse.

I can see his chest moving. He's not dead, he will feel like death when he comes to… "Karma," I scream at his unconscious body. "I'm leaving Carmen and I won't be back."

"He'll find you Am-ori."

"He can try."

I toss a few things from my dresser and bathroom into my bag, then grab my purse. I pull out a twenty and toss it on Alec.

"When he wakes up, tell him the band-aids are on me."

I stop the first taxi I see. When the driver asks me where I'm going, reality sinks in. I have no place to go.

Everyone I know has a connection to Alec.

"Drive me to the main strip, I'll tell you when to stop."

I slip off my shoes and pull a pair of jeans and a t-shirt from my bag. Getting dressed was the last thing on my mind when I was rushing to get out.

Now, I need to figure things out. I have the driver drop me off at The Peppermill. It's a twenty-four-hour restaurant on Las Vegas Blvd... I need time to think. My adrenaline rush has faded and in its place is nerves.

I don't regret doing what I did to Alec, but the thought I could have killed him scares me.

I take a table in the far corner and order a coffee. The waitress lays a menu on the table and I push it aside. My stomach needs to settle, food is the last thing on my mind right now.

Six hundred twenty-seven dollars and thirty-cents. All I have to my name. I need to find a place for the night and a bus schedule. Staying in the city is not an option for me.

After several cups of coffee, I can tell the waitress is getting irritated, so I quickly glance at the menu and order the Bruschetta appetizer and a classic Cobb Salad.

While waiting for my food, I pull out my phone. I have several texts and missed calls.

> **Alec:** *Answer your fucking phone!*
> **Alec:** *You're a dead bitch!*
> **Carmen:** *Alec is flipping the fuck out. He trashed your apartment.*
> **Alec:** *I'm coming for you cunt!*

Carmen: *Run Am-ori! Get out of the state. He will kill you.*

I close out of messages and throw my phone back in my purse.

I need to get a new phone, one of those pre-pay ones.

"Amber."

I jump from the sound of a man's voice saying my name. A tall, muscular guy stands at the end of my table. He looks familiar.

"I knew it was you," he says. "I never forget a face, especially one as beautiful as yours."

"Um… Hi," I know him, but his name eludes me.

"Demetri," he says and sits down across from me. "Andre's friend. Does that jog your memory?"

"Oh, God! Yes!" I say with a little too much excitement.

"What are you doing here alone at…" he looks at his watch. "Two-thirty in the morning?"

Do I need to hide the truth from him?

"I'm just grabbing a quick bite before heading to the bus station."

"Bus station? Are you going on vacation?"

"Not exactly," I take a deep breath. "I'm leaving town… for good."

He raises an eyebrow, giving me a questioning look. He's just about to speak when the waitress shows up with my food.

After setting my plates down, she turns to Demetri.

"Can I get you anything, Sir?"

"Yes, you see the table over there with the three guys? Tell the waitress that handles that table to give you the Denver Omelet. I'll be eating over here."

"No problem. Can I get you a drink?"

"Already have one, thank you."

She turns and heads to the front counter.

"Let me go grab my coffee and tell the guys I'll be eating with you."

"Demetri, you don't have to abandon your friends."

"I'll be right back," he says and walks away towards his group of friends.

Demetri and I ate our food and talked a lot about nothing. Just random conversation. It was nice.

"Well, I should get going. I've kept you from your friends long enough."

"They already left," he points back at where they were sitting.

"I'm sorry, why didn't you say something? I feel awful now."

"Amber, I chose to stay with you. Besides, they're big boys, they can get back to the hotel on their own."

"I still feel bad. At least let me pay for your food."

"Not happening. I'll pay and you'll come back to the hotel with me."

"Demetri, no, I can't impose on you or your friends any more than I already have."

"I have my own room, and you're not imposing, I'm offering. It's late, come back to my room, get some rest and in the morning we'll talk about where you are going."

I am tired and I don't have a clue or a plan where I want to go.

"Ok, thank you."

"You're welcome."

He picks up both our checks, then throws cash on the table for a tip.

"I'll go flag down a taxi while you take care of the check."

"Ok, I'll be out in a minute."

I toss my bag over my shoulder and go outside. I see a few taxi's parked and head towards them.

"Ow! What the…"

Someone grabs my hair and pulls me back, a hand covers my mouth and a hard body slams against me.

"I told you I was coming for you, bitch."

Alec! No! No! No! This can't be happening.

"You think I couldn't find you? I've had a tracker on your phone for quite some time. How do you think Tucker just so happen to run into you last night? Now, I'm going to move my hand and you will walk quietly with me over to my car."

The second his hand moves from my mouth, I scream and throw my elbow back into his gut. But it's not hard enough for him to let me go.

"Get your fucking hands off her."

Demetri's voice is loud and full of anger.

"Fuck off," Alec bites back. "This is none of your business."

Alec's body is pulled away from me, and I stumble back.

"I'm making it my business."

Alec's arm lifts, his fist flies forward, but Demetri is fast and catches it mid-swing.

"Mother Fucker!" Alec screams when Demetri bends his wrist back then swings his fist straight into Alec's nose.

"Now, I will only say this once," he bends his wrist back a little further. "Get the fuck out of here and don't let me ever see your fucking face again." Demetri releases his hand and shoves him back. "Go!" he roars.

Alec stands and takes off down the street, shooting me a death glare.

CHAPTER FIFTEEN

TORI

Demetri takes me back to his hotel. We rode in silence.

"Is he the reason you are running?"

He asks once we are in his room.

"Yes."

"Is he the one who put those bruises on your neck?"

"No."

"Amber, what's going on? If he didn't, then who did?"

"Tori, my real name is Tori."

Three hours later and Demetri knows my life story.

"I'm one fucked up girl," I say with a bit of sarcastic humor.

"Come home with me."

"What? No, Demetri, I won't be anyone's burden."

"I can help you, Tori. I'll give you a job and a place to stay. But, before you say yes, let me tell you what I do. I own a place called Club Allure. It's a place men and women can come and live out their sexual fantasies. I provide a safe environment for them where they won't be judged and are free to explore their sexuality."

"Like an escort service? What I do... used to do."

"No, nothing like that. Everything happens within the walls of my club and not just anyone can walk through the doors. Unless they are a member or an approved guest of a member, there's no getting in."

I sit quietly as Demetri tells me all about Club Allure. I have him describe some fantasies to me and my body responds at the thought of all things BDSM.

"It's your choice, Tori. I won't ask you to commit, just come home with me, check out the club and meet some of the women and men that work for me. If you decide you want to give it a chance, then I'll get you set up. But, Tori, whether or not you decide to try it, I still want you to stay with me. I'll help you find another job and when you're on your feet, you can find a place of your own. No burden, no commitment. Just a friend helping a friend."

"I don't know what to say."

"How about yes?"

"Yes! Yes, thank you, Demetri," I wrap my arms around him, squeezing him tight. "Oh, can I use the name Amber? I'd feel more comfortable."

"Of course. Most of the girls use a different name."

"Really?"

"Yes. It's not uncommon. Now, let's get some sleep, then we'll pack up and hit the road."

We slept most of the day… well, I did. It was one of the best night's sleep I've had in a long time. When I woke up, I found Demetri out on the couch with a laptop opened in front of him.

He looks up, "Hey, sleepyhead."

"Hi. Did you get any sleep?"

"A few hours. I will order some dinner before we leave. We have a seven-hour drive ahead of us… give or take, depending on traffic."

"I would help you drive, but my license expired."

"We'll take care of that after you're settled."

"Thank you, Demetri. For everything."

Our drive to his house was relaxing. I had suggested we wait until morning to leave, but Demetri wanted to be back home early. Explaining he wanted to get me settled in at the house, then take me to the club.

His house is not what I was expecting. It's a small ranch, set in the middle of what he said is a one-acre lot.

He gives me a tour and one thing stands out.

"Um… Demetri, you only have one bedroom."

"Yes, I'll sleep in the office. The couch pulls out. Besides, I'm at the club most of the time, I only come home to sleep."

"We can share the bed."

"No, I have a rule. Other than in the club, I never sleep with any of the girls that work for me."

"You will in the club?"

"We put on shows. That is the only exception to my rule. Mixing business with pleasure outside of the club can cause complications and I don't need nor do I want complications… again."

"I understand. But, we can still sleep in the same bed without *sleeping* together."

"Temptation. Another thing I try to avoid. I'll be fine in my office, trust me. Now, we've got a few hours before heading to the club. I'll go clean out some space in the closet for you."

When Demetri said he only comes home to sleep, he wasn't joking, and it's obvious he doesn't cook.

I would make us lunch, but the only thing in the fridge is milk, orange juice, and a package of lunch meat. The freezer wasn't any better, full of frozen box meals. "Yuck, how can anyone eat those?"

"It's bachelor food."

"Shit! I didn't hear you come in."

He laughs at me. "We'll do some shopping tomorrow. In the drawer to your left is the takeout menus. Pick a place, we'll pick food up on the way to the club."

I decide on Italian and we get the family size meal so we can bring the leftovers home.

CHAPTER SIXTEEN

TORI

"Is there a mall near the grocery store? I'd like to get some clothes tomorrow if you don't mind."

"I noticed you only had one bag."

"Yeah, I didn't waste time sorting through clothes. I just grabbed whatever and shoved it in my bag."

"Given the circumstances, I don't blame you. We'll get it taken care of."

"Thank you."

I should feel overwhelmed by everything that has happened. But the fact that I am free of Alec is a relief, and that alone calms me.

I should have run a long time ago, but fear held me, especially with Alec knowing my true identity. It's something I don't expect people to understand... unless they experienced abuse the way I have. My father injected fear in me with every beating and even though I escaped, just the thought of Alec making good on his threat held me under his thumb.

With Demetri, I feel safe.

"We're here."

I look out the window just as Demetri pulls into a parking lot. A big building with no windows sits at the back. There's no sign with the club's name, only an address above what looks to be a solid steel door.

There are a few cars in the lot parked in front of the building and Demetri drives past them and around the back where several more cars are parked.

"All employees enter through the back. The members use the front entrance. I give each one a code specific to their membership, they use that to gain entrance. Same with everyone who works here. I'll get you set up with a passcode tonight."

"Sounds like you run a tight ship."

"A safe ship," he corrects.

We enter a hallway, and I follow Demetri. He opens a door that leads into what I am assuming is his office.

"We'll eat in here, but first let me show you around."

"Each of the rooms are for sexual pleasures."

He opens one of the doors and I'm stunned speechless. Crops, floggers, whips, and things I've never seen before are hanging across one wall. There's a bed on the opposite wall, and straight ahead is a wooden cross with shackles for wrists and ankles.

"Not every room is the same," Demetri explains. "Some are only beds, others have a viewing window. Each member has different needs and fantasies."

"This is… I don't have the words to express my thoughts."

Demetri laughs. "Overwhelming?"

"No, not at all. I feel aroused just imagining all the things that can happen in these rooms."

"You'll have your chance soon. Come, let's go out to the main room."

We go through another door that requires a code. I step into what looks like a theatre… minus the rows of seats. Instead, there are booths along the back and sidewall. Tables and chairs placed in the center, all facing the huge stage.

"What happens up there?" I ask.

"Many things. We do demonstrations. Some members have their fantasies played out."

"Wow. Anyone can use the stage?"

"Yes, they just have to let me know first."

Demetri takes my hand. "You ready to meet some of the girls?"

I didn't even notice the bar in the main room. Demetri pulls a chair out for me, and I hop up.

A swinging door opens to my left and two beautiful women walk behind the bar.

"Demetri, I didn't hear you come in," the blonde one says.

"Haven't been here long. Carrie, Lyla, this is..." he pauses and looks at me.

"Tori," I say to them. "It's nice to meet you."

"I want you girls to give Tori a proper tour tonight. I'd like to have her sit in on a scene."

"We can do that. Lyla and I will be with Chez and Kara."

"Perfect. Are you ok with that, Tori?"

"Yes."

"Good. Let's go eat. Do you girls want to join us? We have plenty."

"We'll use this viewing room. You can watch from behind the glass." Lyla tells me. "That way if you get uncomfortable you can shut the curtain."

I walk over and look at the room on the other side of the glass.

"If it's not for you, go out to the bar. Carrie and I will meet you there when we're finished."

They go into the other room. I watch as they undress. Lyla puts on a black bra that has a cutout for the nipples and a pair of crotchless panties. Carrie has the same outfit, except it's pale blue. Both of them are stunningly beautiful.

Lyla pulls Carrie to her and their mouths meet. Even from behind this window, I can feel the passion in their kiss.

They stop when the door opens.

A tall man with blonde hair and a slim body that looks to be fit walks in with a striking woman that has fire red hair down to her waist and the little green dress she's wearing shows off curves that most women would kill to have.

As soon as the door clicks shut, Lyla and Carrie go straight to the woman while the man takes his clothes off and sits on the chair in the middle of the room.

Lyla and Carrie undress the woman. Each take a nipple, their tongues roll around the peak. The woman's head falls back, her mouth opens, and the moan that fills the room is my own.

This is the hottest fucking thing I've ever seen.

They move to the bed; the woman lays down. Lyla and Carrie devour her from lips to clit. All while the man watches and strokes his cock.

I'm turned on and my hand moves down and into my pants. I rub my clit and slip a finger into my pussy. I get myself off watching them and thinking about when I get to be the one in the other room.

CHAPTER SEVENTEEN

TORI - 2 YEARS LATER

Most people say there's a fine line between pleasure and pain… I'm not most people and my line is not fine… it's bold.

In the past two years here at Club Allure, I've discovered new ways to feed my craving. And the best part is, I don't have to sneak off to find it.

Demetri doesn't control me, but he watches over me… over all of us.

There has been a time or two where Demetri stepped in and stopped my session. One member got carried away a couple of times. The first time I convinced Demetri to give him a warning. The second time, I had no control or say and he tossed the guy out with a bloody face and I ended up with stitches because the guy couldn't control himself or the crop. I was helpless and handcuffed to a suspension bar.

For a while, members were afraid, and our sessions were mild.

I moved out of Demetri's place a month after I got here. Lyla and Carrie talked me into moving in with them.

They had a spare bedroom since the two of them shared one. The three of us have become close.

I didn't open myself up easily to them, but they didn't give up and I gave in. I have to admit, having friends that truly care about me makes me feel good. There's nothing we wouldn't do for one another.

Shortly after arriving here, I looked up my father. Turns out two years after I ran away he was busted for assault. He did a number on Margo and she pressed charges according to the news article and the court documents. When the police went to arrest him, they walked in on a drug fest. It'll be awhile before he gets out of prison.

I had thought about calling Mitch but decided it wouldn't be a good idea. My life is not what it used to be. I'm no longer the sixteen-year-old girl he once knew.

I arrived at the Club early today. I'll be playing out a fantasy on the stage tonight with a husband and wife. They both want to be submissive and left the scene completely up to me.

I ran my idea past Demetri and he gave me the go-ahead.

"You need some help?"

I turn to see Xavier, who is a long-time member here. He has watched me on the stage before. He's even been on the other side of the glass in one of the viewing rooms. But I have yet to be with him. He's usually with two other girls, Sadie and Trista. I've known of a few times he joined Lyla and Carrie.

Xavier has always been sweet to me. We've sat and talked at the bar many times, but that's as far as it's ever gone.

"Sure. You want to bring me that case?" I point to the wall where it's sitting. "You're early today."

"Demetri has some things to take care of. He asked me to be here for a delivery."

He sets the case next to the cross that will be part of the show tonight.

"Thanks."

"Anytime. So, what's the scene for the lovely Mr. and Mrs. Caprey?"

"It's a surprise. I think it will satisfy them both."

"With you Amber, I can't imagine them being anything but satisfied."

Yes, I still use my fake name. Demetri was right, it's not uncommon. Lyla and Carrie use them as well. Before they came to work here, they were strippers at a dive club. They used the names Roxy and Violet and continued to do so here.

The buzzer for the back door goes off.

"Well, that's my cue," Xavier says. "I'll see you soon."

The Caprey's are all set. Keith is naked and strapped to the cross. Liz is kneeling in front of him, also naked aside from the collar around her neck.

They have given me total control and Keith made it clear he wants to experience all sexual avenues with his wife.

"Are you ready?" I ask them and I can hear the excitement in their voices when they both respond *"yes."*

I slip off my dress revealing my outfit, a black leather corset that is cupless to expose my breasts and a pair of lace crotchless panties.

I turn to Demetri and give a nod, his cue to open the curtains.

I have marked Keith and Liz with crops, floggers, and paddles. I have filled them with dildos, plugs, and anal beads.

Keith wanted a full sexual experience, and he got it when I put both Liz and me in a strap-on and put him on all fours so his wife could fuck his ass while I stood in front of him and fucked his mouth.

Everyone in the club went wild with that scene, and Keith and Liz got their fantasy and a lot more.

CHAPTER EIGHTEEN

TORI

After my show with Keith and Liz, the requests for on-stage fantasies started pouring in. Demetri had to limit them to three nights a week.

"Hey, Amber" Lyla sits at the bar and Xavier follows.

"You and C…," I almost slip and use the wrong name. "Violet finished already?"

"Yes, she'll be out here in a few. Xavier wants to talk to the three of us."

I turn in my seat and look over to him.

"What's up? You looking for a foursome?"

His face turns red. It's cute.

"Sort of," he says, surprising me. "I'm bringing my buddy here tomorrow night. He's new to all of this. I was hoping I could get the three of you to meet with him. Give him some choices. See what he likes and dislikes. Would you be cool with that?"

"Count me in," I turn to Roxie (Lyla). "What about you and Violet?"

"We're game, I won't have to ask her."

"Cool," Xavier says. "We'll be here around seven."

"I wonder what Xavier's friend is like," I say to Lyla and Carrie as we set up the room. "Maybe we should start light."

"So, no strap-ons for the guy?" Lyla laughs.

"Ha-ha. Well, it's almost playtime. You girls ready?" I ask them.

We all kneel in the center of the room, facing the door.

A few minutes go by and he walks in with Xavier. He's gorgeous.

"This is Amber, Roxie, and Violet," Xavier says to him. "They're here for your pleasure, Jordon. I told you the rules, everything else is fair game. Have fun, my friend."

Xavier walks out, leaving Jordon alone with us.

"Look at me,"

His voice is deep. I can hear the commanding tone and with that command, I get a good look at him. His hair is tousled like he just ran his fingers through it. His eyes are brown, but I can see flecks of gold.

When he moves over to the bed, he sits then asks us to join him.

"How old are you girls?"

His question surprises me.

That entire evening was a surprise. Jordon talked with us. He wanted to know our desires, our likes, and dislikes. It was strange, but for reasons I can't explain, I opened up to him. As did Lyla and Carrie.

Jordon returned every night that week. We learned much about one another during that time, including the three of us telling him our real names. Something none of us has ever done before.

I don't know what it is about this man, but I'm drawn to him. I put my entire story out in the open. Lyla and Carrie never knew everything until that moment and the look of shock, pity, and hurt flooded their eyes.

Last night when we were getting ready to call it a night, Jordon asked me to stay behind. There was an instant hum that vibrated through me.

This is it. I thought.

Getting to know this man has only made me want him more.

Jordon surprised me again when he pulled me to him and just… held me.

My body hesitated. It wasn't something I was used to.

"I'm sorry," he told me.

He apologized for everything my life had dealt me.

Things have been great since Demetri saved me. Everyone here has been nothing but kind. But Jordon makes me feel different.

I feel cared for. I feel loved.

The girls and I are in the room waiting for Jordon. When he walks in he doesn't come to sit with us like he has been doing every night.

"Kneel," he says.

It takes a second for us to process his word. A single word. A word that just changed the entire scene.

He walks around us. When his fingers touch my shoulder and trace up my neck, my body reacts.

"Stand up, Tori,'

I do as I'm told.

He guides me back, putting distance between me and the girls.

Jordon's hand trails down my chest, over my stomach, and stops between my legs. His finger runs over my panties and across my clit.

"Take these off."

I remove my panties. His finger returns to my clit, he rubs a few circles over it before moving away.

Something moves across my skin, down my spine, and over my ass cheeks.

Smack!

Jordon moves around to my front. The crop glides between my breasts and over my stomach.

Smack!

A hit to my thigh.

He moves close to me. His body pressed up against mine, he tilts my head and his lips slide up my neck to my ear.

"I know you love the pain," he whispers. "I won't hurt you," his finger slips into my pussy and he bites my lobe. "But I will give you pleasure."

CHAPTER NINETEEN

TORI

The girls and I have been with Jordon every night. He's found his place in our world and our hearts.

He loves the control and I love the feeling of security I get when I'm with him.

The sex between us is more than just sex. Our bodies are an instrument and Jordon has fine-tuned each note, giving each one a different level of pleasure and pain.

There are times I try to get Jordon to heighten my pain, especially when my nightmares return.

"Tori," Demetri calls out and makes his way over to me.

"Hey, Demetri,"

"Do me a favor. When Jordon gets here, tell him I need to see him."

"Is everything ok?"

"Just tell him to come and find me."

He turns and walks away. It's rare Demetri looks irritated. I wonder what's going on.

We sit at the bar. All three of us worried.

Jordon has been in Demetri's office for over an hour.

"He still in there?"

Xavier asks and sits on the stool next to me.

"Yes," I down the rest of my drink and slide the glass towards Sadie who's behind the bar.

"I'm sure everything is fine. Jordon's a math whiz, Demetri probably has him crunching numbers."

I laugh at his theory.

"There's that beautiful smile," he tells me.

Xavier keeps us occupied by telling us about his work and how he met Jordon.

"He just walked up to me and started talking construction. The man knows his shit."

"Who knows what shit?"

I turn when I hear Jordon's voice. He smiles at me.

"Hey, is everything ok?"

"Let's go in the back. Xavier, you too."

I turn to Lyla and Carrie; they look worried, like me.

Jordon shuts the door and leans against the wall.

"What's going on man?" Xavier is the first to speak.

"I will be looking for a place. It's time for me to start what I set out to do when I left home. I don't know where I'm going, but I do know I want you girls with me."

"Is that what you and Demetri were talking about?" I ask him.

"Not at first, but in the end… yes. It's completely up to you three. Demetri knows what I'm asking."

"Wow," Xavier says. "Have you thought about where you might want to go?"

"It doesn't matter," I cut in. "I'm going. I'm with you, Jordon."

"Are you sure? You can take some time to think about it."

"I'm positive. I don't need time," I look over at Lyla and Carrie. They look at each other and smile, then turn towards Jordon.

"We are with you," they both say together.

***

Jordon spent the next few weeks researching different areas in and out of state. Narrowing it down to a few places.

He included us with every decision and together we chose the little city with big attractions… Dell Rapids, South Dakota.

Jordon found the perfect piece of land and made the trip to finalize everything while Lyla, Carrie, and I packed up our things and tied up loose ends.

Demetri threw a party for us. He was sad we were leaving but told us he only wants what's best for us and we will always have a place and a home here… and in his heart.

The next day Jordon and I hopped in the U-Haul. Lyla and Carrie were in Jordon's truck and we hit the road heading towards our new home. A new beginning, a new life… together.

CHAPTER TWENTY

TORI - 21 YEARS LATER

Life with Jordon and the girls has been extraordinary. We are a family. A family I used to wish for but never had… until them.

The love I have for Lyla and Carrie isn't the same love they have for one another, but that doesn't make it less. There isn't anything we wouldn't do for each other.

Jordon loves each of us equally. He provides for us in a way most wouldn't understand.

Yes, we kneel for him. Yes, we obey his command. But that's only in the playroom or the shared bedroom.

We all have jobs and not because we have to, but because it's what we want. We don't have to ask permission if there's something we want to do or buy.

We have date nights. Sometimes all four of us, other times Jordon takes us individually.

I love my time alone with Jordon. There's a special connection between us, and my craving for him has masked my need for pain over the years. The need is still there, and sometimes the mask breaks and Jordon has to reel me back… and he always does.

Sometimes I wish I could turn it all off. I hate when my nightmares return and my past haunts me. It brings out a part of me I don't like… the pain, the jealousy.

Neither Jordon nor the girl's fault me for it. They don't give me pity when it happens. They give me patience, time, and most importantly love, even when I'm at my worse.

But last night something shifted. Jordon came home. We were waiting in the playroom, the three of us naked and kneeling. He came into the room and told us he was tired and had a headache.

Something was off. I had seen it in his eyes. I tried several times to get him to talk to me. He told me to leave.

He didn't yell, but the tone was firm, making it loud and clear he wanted to be alone.

Today they went out riding. Lyla asked me to join them, but I wasn't in the mood.

I waited until they were in the stable, then went into the kitchen. I feel awful for how I acted last night. It was selfish of me to not give Jordon his space. Tonight we'll have dinner, and I'll apologize.

Dinner went great and my apology to Jordon went even better.

Now we are in the playroom.

Jordon is in front of Carrie, his dick in her mouth. He grabs her hair and pushes deep into her throat.

My body hums with anticipation, knowing Jordon will be in front of me soon.

When he pulls away from Carrie, I take a deep breath then wet my lips.

"Maria"

The unknown name comes out of Jordon's mouth in a whisper.

I watch in shock as he goes to his knees and pulls Carrie's leg over his shoulder.

When he buries his face in her pussy, she cries out.

Jordon pulls back. He looks confused. He panics and stumbles back. Carrie reaches for him. He pulls away, hurries to his feet and runs out the door.

Anger floods my veins from what I just witnessed. I go after him.

His door hits the wall when I push it open.

"What the fuck was that?" I scream. Lyla grabs my arm. "Don't fucking touch me, Lyla. We deserve an explanation."

Jordon can't even look me in the eyes and fuels my anger.

"Is there someone else Jordon? Are you slipping your dick into another cunt?"

"No."

"Seriously, Jordon? You're going to lie to me now?"

"Tori, I'm not lying."

"Then who the fuck is Maria?"

The look on his face is terror. He puts his head down.

"Carrie get her out of here."

"I'm not going anywhere until he answers me."

Carrie puts her arms around me, pushing me towards the door.

"Who the fuck is Maria?"

"Tori, not now!"

"I want an answer, Carrie. He needs to give me… give us an answer."

"I know, but you need to calm down. Come with me, please."

I give up the fight. Jordon won't look at me. He sits there in silence, and I give in to Carrie and leave the room.

<hr>

I didn't see Jordon all weekend and when I woke up this morning; he had already left.

Lyla and Carrie didn't tell me much about how he was feeling when they came to check on me, and as far as who Maria is, they gave me nothing. All they said is that I need to talk to Jordon.

I know I have to, but the betrayal that I feel hurts and I don't want a repeat of the other night.

But I decide to go to his office, anyway. I know he'll be there, he's working on the spec homes they are putting up.

I pack a lunch for the two of us and head out.

When I arrive at the office, I notice Jordon's truck is not there. Looking around the site, I spot Xavier sitting on a pile of lumber.

"Hey, Tori. What brings you here?" he asks when I sit down next to him.

"Hi. I'm here to see Jordon. Have you seen him?"

"He took off about an hour ago. He should be back soon."

Xavier and I are talking about a big project they have coming up when I hear Jordon's truck.

I turn towards the office and anger boils to the surface when I see the passenger door open and a blonde woman gets out.

They are talking, but then Jordon's hand reaches up and his fingers brush the side of her mouth.

His back is to me, and her focus is on him. Neither one hears me approach.

"Hi," Jordon spins around, a shocked expression on his face.

This must be Maria. Time to find out.

"You must be Maria," she nods and I step around Jordon. "I'm Tori. Jordon was just talking about you the other night."

"Hi, Tori."

I put my hand out and move it up to her face. I feel the slight jump and see the startled, surprised look on her face.

That's right, be afraid, bitch.

I compliment her skin… which is flawless. "You should stop by Rosie's Salon. I do facials, I'd love to give you one," I say to her. "Anyway, I just stopped by to bring my guy's lunch, but I guess it's all yours Xavier." I hand him the cooler and peck him on the cheek.

I then turn to Jordon. His expression hasn't changed and I'm about to turn up the level of his discomfort a notch or two.

I take his arms and pull him down until our faces are close. I put my mouth to him, holding for just a few seconds.

"I'll see you later tonight," I tell him and before I walk away, I turn to Maria. "Hope to see you soon, Maria. I work on Tuesdays and Fridays."

CHAPTER TWENTY-ONE

TORI

Maria showed up at Rosie's the very next day. I found out she'll be staying in town for a while. Turns out the big project Jordon will be doing is for her.

I need to make it clear Jordon is off-limits. To share him with Lyla and Carrie is one thing. Those two have a relationship of their own. Their love for Jordon and me differs from the love they have for each other. Just as my love for Jordon differs from the love I share with Lyla and Carrie.

If Maria accepts my invitation and shows up at the house tonight, she'll receive my message loud and clear.

I spent the day cleaning. I used my lavender-scented spray.

Lyla and Carrie are getting ready in the playroom. I grab the USB that has the playlist of songs that Jordon knows I only listen to when my nightmares return. Playing this will guarantee he will focus on me tonight.

My wrists are cuffed to the suspension bar and Carrie just freed my ankles from the spreader.

Between the nipple and clit clamps and the strikes of the crop and leather strap, my body is buzzing.

Jordon picks my legs up and they wrap around his waist. He thrusts his cock deep and hard into my pussy. It's not long before an orgasm rips through me. I'm just coming down from it when Jordon stops and I smile in my head when I see Maria standing at the door.

She walks towards Jordon. When he goes to speak, she stops him and then proceeds to remove her dress.

What the fuck!

I'm stunned speechless when she kisses him.

The anger pulsing through me vibrates up and out of my mouth to the tone of a deep growl.

Maria turns to me and smiles, and when I see her reach for the crop, my body tightens.

She wouldn't fucking dare.

She doesn't hit me; She does something so shocking the level of it is off the charts.

I gasp along with Lyla and Carrie, but Jordon… Jordon moans and she does it again, cracking the crop against his balls.

As if tonight can get any worse, Maria pushes Jordon to his knees and lifts one of her legs over his shoulder.

The night with Carrie flashes in my head. My hands pull against the cuffs.

Maria turns her head to me, her pussy grinds on Jordon's mouth.

Smack!

Without warning, she cracks the crop on my clit.

Fuck!

My body should not be responding to her, but it betrays me and with the next strike I feel my juices sliding down my legs.

I'm helpless being cuffed to the bar. Lyla and Carrie can't take their eyes off them, especially when Jordon picks Maria up and fucks her against the wall.

I need to get out of here.

My head is screaming, and my heart is hurting.

When Jordon releases her, she walks over to me.

Her finger slips inside my pussy, then she brings it to her mouth before kissing me.

My body responds again. *Fucking traitor.*

When her hands reach up to the cuffs, she moves her mouth close to mine again.

"Honey, you invited me to a game I know all too well how to play."

She kisses me again, then releases my wrists.

Anger, hate, betrayal, pain, lust, and pleasure all collide inside me. My emotions can't handle the overload.

I see the look of satisfaction on Maria's face. I move forward and step around her and go straight for the door.

I hear the knock on my door, but ignore it while I pull clothing out of the drawers. The knock gets louder.

I pull open my door. Jordon asks to come in.

"It's your house, Sir."

"Tori, please."

I scream at him.

"Never, not once in the past twenty-plus years have you allowed any of us to do to you what that woman… that cunt did to you."

"I'm sorry."

That's all he gives me. After all this time, he can only say I'm sorry and it pisses me the fuck off.

"I hate you. I hate you. I hate you!" my fists beat against him and he lets me continue with my assault.

I hate myself for doing this to him. I break down and fall into his embrace.

My tears stream down his chest, and he holds me tight.

After a few words, I say to him the one thing I know to be true.

"You're in love with her." It's not a question, but he answers.

"Yes, I am," he wipes my tears.

"I've felt your distance," I explain to him and he swears to me that until tonight he's never been with her sexually.

And when he describes how Maria makes him feel, I can't help but put my feelings in perspective.

"I love you Jordon, but I've never felt for you what you do for her. I also know I can't stay here."

"Tori, please."

I explain to him I was the one who invited Maria here. I did it to hurt him and to scare her.

I had seen the way he looked at her that day at his office. I should have looked closer and harder. I would have seen how real it was.

"You can't just leave."

"You should go back to Maria."

I cry as I shut the door.

There was a note on my pillow from Jordon this morning.

He wants to have dinner… just the two of us. He wants to talk.

I need time.

I wait until Lyla and Carrie leave, then I pack up most of my things and I leave.

I know where I'm going, but there's one-stop I have to make.

I pull up to the address Maria put down on her customer card at the salon.

It's a cute little cottage. There's a car parked in the driveway. I was taking a chance to come here in the middle of the day. But it's a chance I had to take.

I hesitate briefly before knocking on the door. It takes less than thirty seconds for the door to open. The look on Maria's face when she sees me is indescribable.

"May I come in?"

She steps aside and I go sit on the couch; I don't think I can do this standing up.

"I need to know… do you get the same intense reaction with Jordon as he does with you?"

She sits next to me.

I listen as she explains the feeling she has and I can see it in her eyes… she's in love with him.

I stand up and head towards the door.

"Tori! Wait!" she yells out.

"He's in love with you, Maria," I turn to face her and I apologize about yesterday. "I'm sorry for setting you up the way I did."

"He loves you too, Tori."

Tears fill my eyes. I know he loves me, but it's not the same and I tell her that.

I won't push Jordon out of my life, I don't think that's possible. But I need time.

"You'll never find another man like him. You're a lucky woman, Maria Dregon. Just do me a favor and never forget that."

After I left Maria's I went to Xavier's house. He wasn't home yet, and when he pulled in the drive, it surprised him to see me on his porch.

He didn't ask for an explanation of why I needed to stay with him, and I was thankful for that.

While I was waiting on the porch, I thought of the words I wanted to say to Jordon and when Xavier got in the shower I wrote them all in a letter.

I don't hate Jordon, I'm not even angry anymore. I'm thankful.

Jordon has been my rock for the past twenty-one years. Every time I spiraled downward, he was there to catch me. When my nightmares returned, he was there to hold me.

It's time for me to be strong and fierce, like he always believed I was. It's time for me to find the love I know is out there waiting for me… because Jordon is right. I deserve it.

Xavier took the letter to Jordon for me, and when he returned he had a letter for me.

I read it, and I cried.

I knew Jordon would understand.

CHAPTER TWENTY-TWO

TORI

I've been staying with Xavier for a month now. We hang out in the evenings and all weekend just talking or watching T.V.

I've had a few conversations with Jordon on the phone and through text messages. I'm not ready to see him and he gets that. Lyla and Carrie come to see me a couple of times a week, even though they see me at the salon. Our bond is unbreakable and I honestly can't picture my life without them.

"Are you ready?" Xavier walks in the living room with a bowl of popcorn in his hand.

I watch as he shovels a handful in his mouth, dropping several pieces on the floor.

"What?" he asks as I keep staring at him.

"Can I ask you something?"

"Anything, you know that," he puts the bowl down and takes a seat next to me.

I take a deep breath and ask him a question I've wanted to ask many times before.

"During my time at Club Allure, why didn't you ever want to be with me?"

He turns to face me.

"I wanted to be with you. More than anything, but…"

He sighs.

"But, what?"

"I couldn't do it, Tori. I couldn't do to you the things you liked."

"You were with the other girls. I've seen what you did with them."

"Yes, but those girls weren't you."

"I don't understand."

"Tori, they weren't you. I didn't want to dominate you, I wanted… I wanted to love you. So many times I wanted to tell you, but I never found the courage. Then Jordon come along. I saw how happy he made you and that's all I ever wanted for you, even if it wasn't with me. So I stepped back and locked my feelings away."

"Xavier…" I don't know what to say. My head scrambles words around but nothing makes sense.

"Tori," Xavier takes my hand. "Why do you think I was able to pick up and leave my life behind when Jordon called? Yes, I wanted to help him, but he wasn't the reason I did it. I did it for you."

Xavier leans in and puts his lips to me. The kiss is soft, it's sensual, it's everything. My body awakens in ways it never has before. It feels as if we have flipped a switch.

You know when you turn on some lights you can hear the electrical current? That buzzing noise that happens just before the light brightens the room.

That's what Xavier's kiss feels like. His lips are the current that awakened me, lighting up parts of me that have been cloaked in darkness.

He pulls away and cups my face.

"For me, it's always been you," he tells me.

"Xavier… kiss me again."

<hr>

It's been eighteen months and Xavier's kisses are what I crave now. The need for pain I once held no longer exists.

We have fun in our playroom… well, we've had to tone it down. Being seven months pregnant is exhausting.

Xavier thinks I will give birth to a bodybuilder as big as I am.

I think he may be right.

"Hey, gorgeous," Xavier wraps his arms around me. "I have another present for you."

"You've already given me roses, chocolates, a back massage, and a foot massage. What more could I possibly need?"

"You'll see. Meet me in the bedroom in ten minutes," he kisses me and smacks me on the ass. "Ten minutes."

"Ok, I'll be there in ten, I promise."

He walks out and I pull the plates out of the dishwasher.

Jordon, Maria, Lyla, and Carrie all came over for Valentine's dinner.

My relationship with Jordon is better than ever, he's my best friend and Maria is right there with him.

She and I have become close, she's a part of our family. She and Jordon are getting married... after I have the baby. That was my term when she asked me to be a bridesmaid.

Funny how things turned out. And I wouldn't change a single second, including everything I went through. From my mother abandoning me to the cruel hand of my father, even my time with Alec. The way I see it, without that, I wouldn't be here. If I would have had a perfect life with a loving mother and father, I wouldn't have run away and all that I have now wouldn't exist.

Maybe fate would've stepped in, but it's not a chance I'd ever be willing to take.

Shit! I look at the clock. I run... waddle into the bedroom.

Xavier is sitting on the edge of the bed. I walk over to him.

"So where's this other present?"

"Under the bed. Sit down, I'll get it."

He gets down on the floor, his arm reaches under the bed. After a minute, he pops up on his knee.

He takes my hand in his.

"I will not ask what I already know the answer to," he slips a ring on my finger. "But I will

tell you this," he kisses me. It's soft. It's sensual,
and it's still everything.

"Tori, for me it's always been you."

The End.

Thank you for reading Finding Me. This is one of the hardest books I've written. Tori holds a special place in my heart, and she deserved to have her story told.

I truly hope you enjoyed it and would be so kind as to leave a review.

Much Love,
CK Marie

Acknowledgments

Heather – What can I say that I already haven't said to you with each of my writing adventures? Thank you for always being there for me. Your friendship is everything to me.
I love you!

Arthetta – Getting to know you over the past couple of years has been amazing. Our friendship is true and unbreakable.
I love you!

Michelle – My trouble twin lol! What would my days be like without you? I love the laughter and smiles we bring to one another from afar. Your friendship means the world to me.
Thank you for all that you do.
I love you!

To All The Bloggers – What would us authors do without you? The time and effort you all give to make sure our work is put out there for so many to see. From cover reveals, teasers, release dates… everything and anything that has to do with our books, you wholeheartedly devote your time to us. Thank you for all that you do and your continuous support.

To All The Readers - You are the heart and soul of the book world. Before I published my first book, I had no clue how important readers were to an author.

I am amazed every day with all of you. With every like of an author page or a post, every share, comment, and review. You bring and give so much love to us all. I thank you sincerely and send love to you all!

SOCIAL MEDIA

Facebook Author Page –
@CKMarieRomanceAuthor

Facebook Readers Group –
C.K. Marie's Delicious Desires

Goodreads - https://bit.ly/2nZ3Bny

BookBub - https://bit.ly/2PjRoFG

PLAYLIST

Hurt – Nine Inch Nails
The Abandoning – Love & Death
Break In – Halestorm
Breathe into Me – Red
Hey You – Pink Floyd
Careless Whisper – Seether
Periscope – Papa Roach
All I wanted – Paramore
A Reason To Fight – Disturbed
In The Air Tonight – Non Point
Conflicted – Halestorm
Behind Blue Eyes – Limp Bizkit
Coming Undone - Korn